This LADYBIRD TALE
belongs to

....

Snow White
and Rose Red

Retold by Vera Southgate M.A., B.COM
with illustrations by Yunhee Park

LADYBIRD 🐞 TALES

ONCE UPON A TIME there was a poor widow who lived with her two little girls in a cottage by the edge of a forest.

In front of the cottage was a small garden in which there grew two rose bushes. One bush bore white roses and the other red roses. These rose bushes were older than the little girls who were named after them.

The two children were alike in that they were both good and obedient and always busy and happy. They were quite different in their appearances and in their ways.

One sister was fair-haired and she was rather quiet and gentle. In the summer, she liked to wear a rose from the white rose bush in her hair. She was called Snow White. The other sister was dark-haired. She loved to run about and skip and dance, and she was always lively and gay. She liked to wear a rose from the red rose bush in her hair. Her name was Rose Red.

Snow White and Rose Red were devoted to each other and often vowed that they would stay together as long as they lived. They shared everything and whenever they went out, they walked along hand in hand.

The children spent a good deal
of their time playing in the forest.
None of the wild animals harmed
them; they often came close to the
little girls and seemed to trust them.

The wild hares used to eat from their
hands, the deer grazed beside them
and the stags leaped around them.
The birds sat on the branches nearby,
singing their sweetest songs.

If the children found themselves far
from home as night came on, they
would even spend the night in the
forest. They used to lie down on a bed
of moss and sleep until morning.

No harm ever came to them. Their
mother knew that she need have no
fear for her children when they were
in the forest.

Once, when Snow White and
Rose Red had spent the night in the
forest, they wakened in the morning
to find a beautiful child in a shining
white dress sitting beside them.
The child smiled at them and then
vanished. When the girls looked
around, they found that they had
been sleeping all night close to the
edge of a steep cliff. They would
certainly have fallen over the edge if
they had moved at all.

When they told their mother
about this, she said that the child
they had seen must have been a
guardian angel who watches over
good children.

Snow White and Rose Red kept
their mother's cottage so clean
and tidy that it was a pleasure
to go into it.

Every morning in the summer,
Rose Red gathered a bunch of
fresh flowers and arranged them
in a vase beside her mother's bed.
Among the flowers there was always
one white rose and one red rose
from the bushes in their garden.

Every morning in the winter,
Snow White lit the fire and hung
the kettle over it. The kettle was
made of copper, and Snow White
kept it polished so that it shone
like gold.

In the winter evenings, when
the snow was falling, the mother
and her little girls gathered
round the fire. While the two girls
sat spinning, their mother read
aloud to them from a large book.
Beside them on the floor slept a
white lamb, while a white dove
perched nearby.

Suddenly, one evening, as they were
sitting quietly by the fire,
a loud knock was heard upon
the door.

"Open the door quickly, Rose Red,"
said her mother. "Some poor
traveller must have lost his way."

Rose Red ran and pulled back the
bolt, then flung open the door.

Into the room there walked, not a weary traveller, but a big, black bear. Rose Red ran screaming towards her mother and sister. Snow White hid behind her mother's chair. The lamb began to bleat and the dove woke up fluttering.

"I have not come to hurt you," said the bear in a gentle voice. "I only want to warm myself by your fire, for I am half frozen."

"Poor bear," said the mother. "Come in and lie down by the fire but take care not to burn your furry coat."

Then she called to her children, "Snow White! Rose Red! You need not hide, for the bear will do you no harm."

So the children came timidly towards the fire and the lamb and dove drew nearer.

Soon, they had lost all their fear and the bear had become their playmate. When bedtime came the mother said, "Stay here by the fire all night, gentle bear." He stayed until the morning came.

Eventually, the children grew so fond of him that at night the door was never fastened until their friend had arrived. Then they used to play together in front of the fire. The children would pull the bear's hair and put their feet upon his back and roll him over. When he growled at them, in fun, they laughed and rolled over with him.

The bear's nightly visits continued until the spring. Then one morning the bear said, "Now that spring is here I must leave you and I shall not return all summer."

"Why must you leave us, dear bear, and where will you go?" asked Snow White.

"I must stay in the forest, to guard my treasures from the wicked dwarfs," replied the bear.

As the bear passed through the doorway, a piece of his fur caught on the latch. Snow White thought she saw a glimpse of gleaming gold beneath the fur, but she could not be certain. The little girls knew they would miss their friend dearly.

Some time afterwards, the children were in the forest gathering firewood. They came to a large tree lying on the ground. Something was jumping backwards and forwards over the trunk of the tree.

As they came nearer, they saw that it was a tiny dwarf with an old withered face and a long, white beard. He had tried to split the tree trunk with his little axe, and his long beard had become trapped. He tugged furiously at his beard but he could not pull it free.

When the dwarf caught sight of Snow White and Rose Red, he shouted, "You ugly creatures! Why do you stand there staring instead of trying to help me?"

The little man was very rude, but the sisters still tried to help. But his beard was stuck firmly in the tree.

Rose Red said, "I will run home and find someone to help you."

"You silly goose!" screamed the dwarf. "What is the use of asking other stupid creatures to stare!"

"Let me see what I can do," said Snow White. She took her scissors and cut the dwarf's beard close to the tree trunk, so that he was free.

The dwarf picked up a bag of gold. Instead of thanking the girls, all he said was, "You wicked children! How dare you cut off a piece of my beautiful beard. Bad luck on you!"

Another day, some time later, Snow White and Rose Red went fishing. In the distance they saw a little figure hopping up and down, as if it were about to jump into the stream. They ran forward and found that it was the dwarf again.

"What are you trying to do?" asked Rose Red. "Surely you don't want to jump into the water?"

"I am not such a fool," screamed the dwarf. "Can't you see that this huge fish is dragging me into the stream?"

The sisters looked and saw that the little dwarf had hooked a large fish on the end of his fishing line. Unfortunately, at the same time his beard had become entangled with the line.

The children grasped hold of the dwarf, but they could not disentangle his beard from the fishing line.

Snow White took out her scissors and cut more of his beard. The dwarf knew that she had done this to save his life, but he flew into a rage.

"How dare you disfigure me in this way?" he screamed. "First you cut off the end of my beard and now you cut off half of it. How can I let people see me when I look such a fright? I hope you have to run until you have no soles left on your shoes!"

Then he picked up a bag of pearls that he had hidden among the rushes, swung it over his shoulder, and disappeared.

Some time afterwards, Snow White and Rose Red were sent to town by their mother to buy needles and thread. Their road led them across a bare stretch of track strewn with boulders of rock. There they noticed a large bird hovering over a certain spot. Suddenly the bird swooped down and the children heard pitiful cries.

They rushed forward and saw with horror that a huge eagle had the dwarf in his talons and was about to carry him off. Snow White and Rose Red caught hold of the little man's coat-tails and hung on with all their might. They pulled so hard that at last the eagle dropped the dwarf and flew away.

As soon as the dwarf had recovered from his fright, he turned on the sisters. "You clumsy clots!" he raged. "What do you mean by handling me so roughly? You have nearly torn my new coat off my back. Could you not have handled me more carefully?"

Then he picked up a sack of precious stones and disappeared behind one of the large boulders.

Snow White and Rose Red were by now used to his rudeness and did not expect thanks for their help. They went on their way to town, where they bought the needles and thread for their mother.

On their way home in the evening, they came across the dwarf once more, in the same place. He was kneeling on the ground, gazing at all his jewels, which were spread around him. The jewels sparkled and gleamed with such fire that the children thought they had never seen anything so beautiful. They could not help but stand and stare.

Suddenly the dwarf looked up. "What are you standing there gaping at?" he yelled and his face grew bright red with anger.

At that moment, a terrible growl was heard and a big black bear came shuffling out of the forest towards them.

The dwarf sprang to his feet, terrified. His angry, red face became white with fear. Before the dwarf had time to escape, the bear was beside him.

Then the dwarf, in a shaky voice, pleaded, "Dear Mr Bear, please spare my life – I beg of you. I am so small, I would only be a mouthful for you to eat. If you are hungry, why don't you eat these two wicked girls? They are much plumper than I am. If you spare me, then I will give you all my treasure."

But the bear paid no attention to the words of the dwarf. He just lifted his fore-paw and with a single blow the dwarf lay dead on the ground.

The little girls were running off in fright, when the bear called after them, "Snow White and Rose Red, don't be afraid. Don't you know me?" The children recognized, with delight, the voice of their dear friend. They turned and ran towards him as he came trotting to meet them.

As they met, his fur fell from him and, instead of a shaggy bear, there stood before them a handsome young man, dressed in cloth of gold.

"I am a king's son," he said. "That wicked dwarf robbed me of all my treasure and put a spell on me so that I was changed into a bear. Ever since then I have wandered through the forest, waiting for a chance to kill him. Not until he was dead could the spell be lifted from me. Now I am free and he has received his just punishment."

Snow White and Rose Red were overjoyed when they heard this tale, as was their mother when the prince went home with them.

A few years afterwards, Snow White married the prince and Rose Red married his brother. The two princes shared the treasure, which the dwarf had hidden for so long.

They all lived happily together in a large castle. The mother of Snow White and Rose Red went to live with them. In the castle garden, below her window, were planted the two rose bushes from her cottage garden. Every summer they bore the most beautiful white and red roses, just as they had done before.

A History of
Snow White and Rose Red

The story of *Snow White and Rose Red*
is one of the lesser-known fairy tales.
It was collected by the Brothers Grimm
in Germany in the 19th century.

The message of the story is simple.
If you are kind and good, like
Snow White and Rose Red, then
you shall be rewarded and loved.
If you are mean, like the wicked
dwarf, then you will be punished.

The Grimms based it on an earlier,
much shorter story called
The Ungrateful Dwarf, written
by Caroline Stahl in 1818.

The Snow White in this story
should not be confused with
the girl of the same name in
the famous Grimm tale
Snow White and the Seven Dwarfs.

Ladybird's 1969 retelling of the story by
Vera Southgate is one of the best-known
versions of *Snow White and Rose Red*
in modern times.

Collect more fantastic
LADYBIRD 🐞 TALES

Little Red
Riding Hood

9781409311126

Goldilocks
and the
Three Bears

9781409311119

Cinderella

9781409311072

Jack
and the
Beanstalk

9781409311102

The
Gingerbread
Man

9781409311096

The Three
Little Pigs

9781409311089

The Three Billy
Goats Gruff

9781409311065

Pinocchio

9780723271062

Puss in Boots

9781409311225

Rapunzel

9781409311195

Rumpelstiltskin

9781409311164

The Elves and the
Shoemaker

9781409311188

Snow White
and the
Seven Dwarfs

9781409311171

The
Enormous
Turnip

9781409311218

The Magic
Porridge Pot

9781409311201

Sleeping
Beauty

9781409311157

The **Princess**
and the **Frog**

9780718192556

Dick
Whittington

9780718192532

The
Big Pancake

9780718192549

Beauty
and the **Beast**

9780718192587

The **Little**
Red Hen

9780718192525

The **Ugly**
Duckling

9780718193133

The **Princess**
and the **Pea**

9780718192570

Chicken
Licken

9780718192563

The **Emperor's**
New Clothes

9780723271048

The **Little**
Mermaid

9780723271055

Hansel
and **Gretel**

9781409311133

Aladdin

9780723271079

Peter
and the **Wolf**

9780723294481

Snow White
and **Rose Red**

9780723294474

Endpapers taken from series 606d,
first published in 1964

A catalogue record for this book is available from the British Library

Published by Ladybird Books Ltd
80 Strand London WC2R 0RL
A Penguin Company

001

© Ladybird Books Ltd MMXV

ISBN: 978-0-72329-447-4

Printed in China